Native
American
Peoples

# SEMINOLE

D. L. Birchfield

**Gareth Stevens Publishing**
A WORLD ALMANAC EDUCATION GROUP COMPANY

Please visit our web site at: www.garethstevens.com
For a free color catalog describing Gareth Stevens Publishing's list of high-quality books
and multimedia programs, call 1-800-542-2595 (USA) or 1-800-387-3178 (Canada).
Gareth Stevens Publishing's fax: (414) 332-3567.

Library of Congress Cataloging-in-Publication Data

Birchfield, D. L., 1948-
    Seminole / by D. L. Birchfield.
        p. cm. — (Native American peoples)
    Summary: A discussion of the history, culture, and contemporary life of the
Seminole Indians.
    Includes bibliographical references and index.
    ISBN 0-8368-3668-5 (lib. bdg.)
    1. Seminole Indians—History—Juvenile literature.  2. Seminole Indians—Social
life and customs—Juvenile literature.  [1. Seminole Indians.]  I. Title.  II. Series.
E99.S28B47    2003
975.9004'973—dc21                                                    2002191131

First published in 2003 by
**Gareth Stevens Publishing**
A World Almanac Education Group Company
330 West Olive Street, Suite 100
Milwaukee, WI  53212  USA

Produced by Discovery Books
Project editor: Valerie J. Weber
Designer and page production: Sabine Beaupré
Photo researcher: Rachel Tisdale
Native American consultant: Robert J. Conley, M.A., Former Director of Native American
    Studies at Morningside College and Montana State University
Maps and diagrams: Stefan Chabluk
Gareth Stevens editorial direction: Mark Sachner
Gareth Stevens art direction: Tammy Gruenewald
Gareth Stevens production: Jessica L. Yanke

Photo credits: Native Stock: cover, pp. 4, 9 (bottom), 10, 11 (bottom), 12, 13, 15, 16, 17 (top),
18 (both), 19, 20 (both), 21, 22, 23, 24, 25, 26; Corbis: pp. 5, 11 (top); Peter Newark's American
Pictures: pp. 6, 14; North Wind Picture Archives: pp. 7, 8, 9 (top), 17 (bottom).

Printed in the United States of America

1 2 3 4 5 6 7 8 9 07 06 05 04 03

Cover: This young Seminole girl in traditional dress stands next to cypress trees.

# Contents

Chapter 1: Origins . . . . . . . . . . . . . . . . . . . . . 4

Chapter 2: History . . . . . . . . . . . . . . . . . . . . 6

Chapter 3: Traditional Way of Life . . . . . . . . 14

Chapter 4: Today . . . . . . . . . . . . . . . . . . . . 22

Time Line . . . . . . . . . . . . . . . . . . . . . . . . 28

Glossary . . . . . . . . . . . . . . . . . . . . . . . . . 29

More Resources . . . . . . . . . . . . . . . . . . . . 30

Things to Think About and Do . . . . . . . . . . 31

Index . . . . . . . . . . . . . . . . . . . . . . . . . . . 32

Words that appear in the glossary are printed in **boldface** type the first time they appear in the text.

# Origins

A Florida Seminole man in traditional dress. This style of clothing was worn by Florida Seminoles from about 1700 to about 1830.

ALABAMA

UNITED
STATES

GEORGIA

Atlantic
Ocean

FLORIDA

Gulf of
Mexico

N

W—E

S

miles
0          125

0      125
km

## The Land of the Seminoles

The Seminoles (SEH-muh-noles) are a North American Native people who separated in the 1700s from a large **nation** of Southeastern Indians called Muscogees (who are also known as Creeks). Their historic homelands include present-day Georgia and Alabama. Today, about ten thousand Seminoles live on four main reservations in Florida or in the Seminole Nation in Oklahoma.

No one knows exactly how the Seminoles and other Native Americans came to North America. Like many Native cultures, however, the Seminoles have, for centuries, told a story to explain how they arrived on the continent. The Seminole origin story tells of a time, long ago, when the tribe emerged from a cave deep beneath the earth. They arrived in their homeland in the Southeast after a long journey from the west.

Some scholars have suggested that Indians might have come to North

The Indian people now known as the Seminoles lived in Florida by the end of the eighteenth century.

America from Asia thousands of years ago during the Ice Age, if there had been a landmass between Asia and Alaska at that time. Others think that Native Americans might have traveled from Asia by boat along the coast of the Pacific Ocean.

## Mound-Building Ancestors

The Muscogees and Seminoles are descended from a great civilization of **mound builders** in the woodlands east of the Mississippi River. Today, state parks in Georgia and Alabama preserve some of those historic earthen mounds.

The Seminole people say that their name is a word in their own language, meaning "a free people." Non-Seminoles have often assumed that the name comes from a Spanish word, *cimarron,* meaning "wild."

The base of Monks Mound at Cahokia in Illinois is larger than the Great Pyramid's base in Egypt.

# History

## Life in the New Land

After the Spanish claimed Florida in 1585, European diseases and war between Spain and England wiped out the original Indian people of Florida. During the 1700s, Muscogees from present-day Georgia and Alabama began moving to that empty land in northern Florida, which was still Spanish territory. By 1775, they had formed a separate tribe in northern Florida, known as Seminoles.

The Seminoles enjoyed a good life as farmers and ranchers. Their population increased to about six thousand as small groups of Indians from other southeastern tribes joined them.

Runaway black slaves sought refuge among the Florida Seminoles. The former American slaves became important allies of the tribe.

## Slaves and Seminoles

The Seminoles also welcomed the many African-American slaves who ran away from the English colonies and joined them. Although some became slaves of the Seminoles, they were treated differently — and better — than slaves in the colonies. Others married Seminoles and became members of the tribe. Some former slaves even formed villages near the Seminoles and became farmers and cattle ranchers like the Seminoles.

The slave owners in Georgia, on the northern border of Florida, however, tried to recapture their runaway slaves by invading Florida in the early 1800s. When the Seminoles resisted those efforts, war broke out between the Seminoles and the

This painting portrays Seminoles in battle. The fighting occurred in 1817 near Fort Scott in Florida.

Georgians. In 1815, General Andrew Jackson helped the Georgians by ordering the U.S. Army to attack the Seminoles in Florida.

In 1819, Spain sold Florida to the United States, and in 1821, large numbers of Americans began moving to Florida under the protection of the U.S. Army. The Seminoles were forced to leave their farms and flee south. Once again, they were a people on the move, but this time they were leaving the rich farmland of northern Florida for a very different kind of environment in central and south Florida.

## The "Battle of Negro Fort"

On July 27, 1816, a tragedy occurred in the war between the U.S. Army and the Seminoles for control of northern Florida. A U.S. gunboat sailed up the Apalachicola River to a Seminole fort and fired a cannon ball that had been heated red hot in hopes of setting fire to the fort. It landed in the fort's gunpowder storage area and blew the whole place to pieces. In an instant, the explosion killed about three hundred African-American men, women, and children and about thirty Seminoles.

# Life in the Swamps

The land in central Florida was not as well suited to farming and cattle raising as northern Florida had been. The Seminoles had to change their way of life and rely more on hunting and fishing.

With some of the largest swamps on Earth, southern Florida was an even bigger change of environment. The Florida **Everglades** are a huge area of tall grass growing out of shallow water, with small islands hidden among the glades.

A Seminole village in the Everglades. The U.S. Army had great difficulty finding the Seminoles in the vastness of the Everglades.

# The Seminole Wars

However, the Seminoles would not be allowed to live in peace in their new homes. In 1830, the United States passed the Indian **Removal** Act and demanded that all Seminoles leave Florida and move to the West. Some Seminoles signed the Treaty of Paynes Landing in 1832, and they were removed to Indian Territory (which later became Oklahoma).

Led by Osceola and Wildcat, however, some Seminoles refused to be removed — they went to war. The war lasted from 1835 to 1842 and became the costliest Indian war — in both money and men — in U.S. history. Many Seminoles were killed, and it cost the

8

> I am an Indian—
> A Seminole! . . . I will
> make the white man red
> with blood, and then
> blacken him in the sun
> and rain, where the wolf
> shall smell of his bones,
> and buzzard live
> upon his flesh.
>
> *Osceola, 1835*

This painting portrays the U.S. Army capturing Seminole chiefs during the war.

United States more than $20 million and the lives of fifteen hundred U.S. soldiers. A few hundred Seminoles were able to hide in the swamps, until, finally, the army gave up trying to remove them.

Another Seminole war broke out in 1855, lasting until 1858, but again the U.S. Army was not able to defeat the Florida Seminoles. They would remain in Florida, separated from most of the tribe that was now in Indian Territory.

## Osceola

Osceola (1804–38) became the most famous Seminole war chief in the war of 1835–42 in Florida. His leadership of the Seminoles in battle caused the U.S. Army great frustration and the loss of many men. Unable to defeat him, the army used deceit to capture him, seizing him when he attended a **negotiation** under a white flag of **truce** in 1837. He was sent to prison in South Carolina, where he died the following year.

Seminole chief Osceola showed his contempt for one U.S. treaty proposal by stabbing the paper with his knife.

The Trail of Tears. Seminoles suffered great hardships and many deaths during their forced removal from Florida to Indian Territory.

## Seminole Removal: A Trail of Tears

The removal of the Seminoles, and the other Southeastern tribes (Choctaws, Muscogees, Chickasaws, and Cherokees), during the 1830s is one of the cruelest episodes in U.S. history. Their journey from Florida to Indian Territory is known as the "Trail of Tears" because so many Native people died. The U.S. government did not provide adequate food, clothing, shelter, or medical supplies during the removal. Weakened by hunger and cold, the Seminoles fell victim to illness as they were moved north during the winter from the warm climate they were used to.

The Seminoles were not all forced from Florida at once. At first, only the Seminoles who had agreed to the removal treaty were removed. Later, during the war, other groups of Seminoles were removed as they were captured by the U.S. Army. Some Seminoles tried to avoid removal, and the warfare in Florida, by fleeing to Mexico. They became unhappy there, however, and within a few years they joined their tribe in Indian Territory.

A black Seminole woman named Hannah in Florida in 1925. She was thought to have been about 105 years old at that time and the only living survivor of the Seminole wars of the nineteenth century.

By the time the last Seminole war ended in 1858, most Seminoles had been removed from Florida. Only two or three hundred managed to avoid removal and stay in Florida.

## Seminoles after Removal

The Seminoles who remained in Florida became a nearly forgotten people during the

## Black Seminoles

The former African-American slaves who had joined the Seminoles in Florida fought valiantly against the United States with their Seminole allies. In 1849, however, led by John Horse (also known as Juan Caballo), they fled to the border region of Mexico and Texas. Some of them joined the U.S. Army and became famous as the "Seminole Negro Scouts," under their leader, Sergeant John Kibbetts. After the American **Civil War**, many of them again served in the army. Today, many of their descendants live near Brackettville, Texas, near the border with Mexico.

An actor portraying a Seminole Negro scout. The Black Seminole soldiers gained fame on the Western frontier as scouts for the U.S. Army.

last half of the nineteenth century and for much of the twentieth century. They survived mostly by hunting and fishing in southern Florida in the Big Cypress Swamp, near Lake Okeechobee, or in the Everglades.

The U.S. government forced the Seminoles who were removed to Indian Territory to once again become a part of the Muskogee (Creek) Nation. Conditions in the Muskogee Nation after removal were horrible. The United States government failed to supply the food and farming equipment it had promised. The government officials who were supposed to provide the food stole the money and gave the Indians barrels of spoiled bacon instead.

## The Civil War Takes a Toll

The Seminoles suffered great hardship again during the American Civil War of 1861 to 1865, when armies from both sides plundered Indian Territory, raiding farms and stealing food and livestock. The war divided the Seminole people as it did the people of the United States. Seminole soldiers fought in both the **Union** and **Confederate** armies during the war.

Seminole men, women, and children after confinement to reservation life in Florida. Most Seminoles were removed to Indian Territory, but a few hundred were able to hide in the swamps and avoid removal.

An early photo of the Seminole town of Wewoka in Indian Territory. The Seminoles in Indian Territory watched helplessly as American settlers crowded in among them and eventually took away their land.

Finally, after the Civil War, the Seminoles in Indian Territory were allowed to separate from the Muscogees and form the Seminole Nation. They created a school system and became prosperous farmers, until non-Native Americans once again began pouring into their lands in 1870s and 1880s, demanding Indian land for themselves.

When the state of Oklahoma was formed in 1907, the Seminoles were forced to become citizens of the new state and to give up their nation and all their land, except for small individual farms. In 1935, however, the Seminoles in Oklahoma were allowed to form a limited government. Finally, in the 1970s, they were allowed to adopt a **constitution** and form the Seminole Nation of Oklahoma, so they might govern themselves.

## Wildcat

Wildcat (1810–57) was a famous Seminole war leader during the war of 1835 to 1842 in Florida. Captured with Osceola and sent to prison with him, Wildcat made a daring escape and continued fighting. When captured again, he was sent to Indian Territory in 1841. Unhappy with conditions there, he led his band of Seminoles to Mexico, where he died in 1857.

# Traditional
# Way of Life

## Traditional Culture

Seminole culture is matrilineal, meaning that people's family tree is traced through the mother's line, rather than the father's as in European-American culture. Seminole culture is also matrilocal, meaning that when a man and a woman get married, they live with the wife's extended family and the children are automatically members of the wife's **clan**.

These arrangements avoid many problems that are common in other cultures. First, spouse abuse is much less common because a wife is surrounded by her male relatives. Second, problems or

These Seminole women in Florida are making cornmeal. They remove the corn from the cob and then pound it into a coarse powder with a  stick.

A young Seminole boy in traditional dress. Seminole women are proud of the skill it takes to make clothing like this.

uncertainties regarding child **custody** in the event of a divorce are also avoided. Because the children are members of the wife's clan, the children stay with the mother in the event of a divorce.

## Seminole Uncles

Seminole children receive much of their training from their uncles, especially the brothers of their mother. The role of uncle is an important one in Seminole culture — uncles have more responsibility in raising a child than the parents. Parents are believed to be too emotionally close to their children to be able to see what might be best for a child. The children benefit greatly, surrounded by relatives who care about them very much.

## Colorful Clothing

Seminole women have developed styles of clothing that are among the most distinctive of all the Indians in North America. They use patches of cloth, sewn together in strips of alternating color and pattern, to make shirts and dresses that are both striking and colorful. Grandmothers and mothers teach this craft to young Seminole girls, who take great pride in learning this very distinctive method of making clothing.

## Seminole Watercraft

The Seminoles in Florida developed great skill in the art of building boats that were suited to their environment. For the shallow water of the Everglades, they fashioned a tree log into a long, narrow, lightweight craft. They propelled the craft by standing in the back of the boat and pushing it through the water with a long pole. For deep water, they hollowed out big logs with fires and made dugout canoes that they used to travel on the ocean, going as far as the islands of the Bahamas off Florida's eastern coast.

## Changing Environment, Changing Lives

The Seminole people have proven to be very adaptable to changing conditions and different environments. When they first settled in northern Florida, their lives were not much different from what they had been among the Muskogees. They planted fields of corn, beans, and squash, and they raised cattle, hunted, and fished.

When they were driven from northern to central and southern Florida, however, they found themselves in an environment not as well suited to agriculture or raising cattle. Even if the land had been more suitable to their former lifestyle, their cattle and their agricultural fields would have been easy targets for the large U.S. armies that hunted them.

The Seminoles survived by adapting to the vastness of the water-covered Everglades and the big swamps nearby. They learned how to harvest the edible plants in the new environment, learned how to depend more on fishing than on hunting, and learned how to find the small islands in the swamps where they could build their houses.

# Chickee

The Seminole chickee is well suited to the environment of southern Florida. This style of house is built on a platform a few feet above the ground to protect it against flooding. An open-sided structure with no walls, the chickee allows cooling breezes to flow through the house. The roof is thatched with leaves from the palmetto plant, providing a deep, cool shade and protection from the rain. The structure can be built quickly, from materials readily at hand.

The Everglades' environment made it very difficult and very costly for the U.S. Army to find the Seminoles. They became very skilled at laying **ambushes** for the soldiers, blending into the vegetation until it was too late for the soldiers to realize they had entered a trap.

The environment also made it more difficult for the Seminoles to carry on their traditional form of government, which had been organized into villages. In the swamps, the people had to become more scattered, living in extended family groups much smaller than their former villages and relying on the leadership of the family elders.

These Seminoles are transporting lumber into the Everglades. The lumber was salvaged from a shipwreck on a nearby ocean beach.

Stickball is still played today. These modern Seminoles are playing stickball at the Big Cypress Reservation in Florida.

## Seminole Sports and Games

The Seminoles are so well known in history for the Seminole wars — and for the fact that they are the only Indian tribe that the United States went to war against but was unable to defeat — that they have gained an image as a warlike people. That image does not accurately portray the richness of Seminole life and the true character of the Seminole people, which can be seen in the tremendous importance they place on sports and games.

## A Seminole Story

Seminoles love telling stories about the animal world. One story tells about a great ballgame that was played by the birds against the four-footed animals. However, no one could decide which team the bat should be on, and at first both teams rejected this flying mammal. After much debate, the four-footed animals allowed the bat to play for them. In the game, the bat led the four-footed animals to a great victory.

Like all the southern Indians, and like many other Indians on the continent, Seminoles loved the game of **stickball**, which European-Americans adopted, calling it lacrosse. The game is still played today but not on the scale of former days.

The big stickball games, called "match games," in which men competed against men, were events that held the entire tribe spellbound, with village competing against village in a frenzied effort that made a lasting impression on all outsiders who witnessed it. Often, the people would bet nearly all of their worldly possessions on a game of ball. Women and men of all ages competed together in other stickball games.

## An Active People

The Seminoles had many other leisure activities and games, including the hoop and pole game, where one person rolled a hoop and the other person tried to hit it with a spear. Footraces were also very popular. They provided **endurance** training for the children and were a way for men and women to stay in good physical condition.

Today, Seminoles still place great value on rigorous athletic activity. Their sports teams for both men and women, particularly softball, play with great enthusiasm and skill.

## Seminole Beliefs

After several centuries of attempts to suppress them by outsiders and the U.S. government, traditional Seminole religious beliefs and

A young Seminole boy competes at archery. With such weapons, the Seminole warriors were able to remain undefeated by the U.S. Army during the nineteenth century.

This traditional Seminole medicine man is carrying a gourd rattle in his right hand, an ancient part of ceremonial rituals.

On the Seminole Reservation in Florida, a Seminole sells ingredients for traditional Seminole medical remedies.

worldview remain strong. From the Seminole viewpoint, humans are merely one of the many creatures on Earth, and all creatures have dignity and a spirit that must be respected. Traditional Seminoles try to live in harmony with the natural world. Many of their beliefs come from traditional stories, and many of those stories tell lessons about how to live in the world that they have learned from various animals.

Seminole religious and cultural beliefs are rich with stories of animals and humans sharing the world together and having an influence on each others' lives. It's not possible to understand how the Seminoles view the world and their place in it without long exposure to the stories and the lessons they teach.

Seminoles and many other Indian tribes are not particularly interested in whether or not outsiders understand their religions. Many Indians

regard inquires about their religions as unwelcome questions about their personal and private lives because most Indian religions do not attempt to convert other people to their beliefs.

## Medicine Men

**Medicine men** continue to be important in Seminole life. They possess the detailed knowledge of the healing powers of herbs and other remedies and carefully preserve the knowledge of magic formulas and ceremonies that the people rely upon to maintain both their health and their sense of well-being in the world.

The most important religious event is the annual Green Corn Ceremony. This event lasts four days in Oklahoma and seven days in Florida, in late June or July, when Seminoles camp together, play ball, and participate in dances, feasts, and religious rituals.

This woman is performing the Fancy Shawl Dance at the Seminole Tribal Fair Powwow.

## Grave Houses

Many Seminoles continue the cultural tradition of covering the grave with a small grave house. The grave houses are about 3 feet (1 meter) high and about 6 feet (2 m) long. The sides of the houses look somewhat like a picket fence. They are found in Seminole cemeteries near the towns of Wewoka and Seminole in Oklahoma.

# Today

## Seminoles Today in Florida

The U.S. government formally recognized the Seminole Tribe of Florida as a separate Indian tribe in 1957. Today, members of the tribe number about three thousand and occupy four main reservations and three very small ones.

At 42,730 acres (17,300 hectares), Big Cypress Reservation is the largest of the federal reservations and is located on the northeastern edge of the Big Cypress Swamp in southern Florida. The Brighton Reservation has 35,800 acres (14,500 ha) and is located northwest of Lake Okeechobee. The Seminole (or Hollywood) Reservation near the city of Miami has only 480 acres (1,190 ha).

The Miccosukee Reservation is another reservation, located in the Everglades about 25 miles (40 kilometers) west of Miami. About four hundred Seminoles live on the Miccosukee Reservation, which was created in 1962, when the Miccosukee Tribe of Indians of Florida gained recognition by the U.S. government as a separate tribe. Indians from more than forty tribes attend their Florida Annual Indian Arts Festival each winter, which features dancing, singing, and exhibits of arts and crafts.

This Seminole farmer is harvesting sugarcane on the Big Cypress Reservation in Florida.

## Governing the Reservations

Each of the reservations in Florida is governed by its own elected council. Those councils meet as a group each year at the Green Corn Ceremony. The councils have created tribal business activities, including tobacco shops, casinos, and cattle-ranching operations.

During the last half of the twentieth century, many Seminoles have preferred modern housing to the traditional chickee. They have built schools for their children and community centers and health-care facilities for the tribe. Their biggest concern is trying to acquire more land for their people while continuing to improve their quality of life.

## Alligator Wrestling

Seminoles in Florida have become famous for entertaining tourists by wrestling the large Florida alligators at small, roadside entertainment centers and at exhibitions on the reservations.

Seminoles at the Miccosukee Reservation are particularly well known for their skill in wrestling the large, dangerous creatures. The alligators are not harmed, and the Seminole wrestlers are rarely injured.

Alligator wrestling on the Miccosukee Reservation in Florida. The Seminole alligator wrestlers are a popular tourist attraction and a source of tourist money for the tribe.

These maps show the locations of the main Seminole reservations in Florida and the Seminole Nation of Oklahoma.

## Seminoles Today in Oklahoma

Today, there are about seven thousand members of the Seminole Nation of Oklahoma. The capital of their nation is located in Wewoka, Oklahoma.

The Seminoles have provided an outlet for their artists and craftspeople to sell their products at the Seminole Nation Museum, also in Wewoka. There, Seminole women display the high level of skill required in making their distinctive patchwork clothing, while men skilled at making the sticks used in stickball games offer them for sale. The sticks are made of slender, finely crafted pieces of hickory.

Seminole basket making, which requires great skill, is a craft handed down from generation to generation.

## An Oil-Rich Land

The Seminoles in Oklahoma should be among the wealthiest Indian tribes in the United States since it was on their land that the great Oklahoma oil boom took place in the early decades of the twentieth century. However, most Seminoles were cheated out of their land by corrupt politicians, lawyers, and judges. The **fraud** took place on a huge scale, and the Seminoles were helpless to do anything about it. Now many Seminoles live near the poverty level.

The Seminoles govern themselves with an elected tribal council. They operate tribal businesses, including tobacco shops that do not have to pay Oklahoma state taxes. They provide educational programs for their children, health-care programs for the tribe, and community centers that give tribal members a place to meet and socialize.

Led by a medicine man, these Seminole young people are preparing to perform a Stomp Dance.

## Seminole Nation Days

Seminole Nation Days, an annual celebration of Seminole culture in Oklahoma, is held each year in September in Seminole, Oklahoma. The event features Seminole arts and crafts, lots of food, visiting with old friends, and traditional Seminole dancing. Many Seminoles who now live outside the Seminole Nation in east-central Oklahoma plan their vacation around the event. Thus, it serves as a homecoming each year for many members of the tribe.

The tribe's most important goal is to keep its tribal sovereignty, which is the right of the tribe to govern itself. To do this, tribal members must be aware of changes in how the U.S. government is handling Indian affairs. They must also guard against state officials who might wish to take away the power and independence of Indian tribes in Oklahoma.

## Contemporary Seminole Leaders

Seminoles have produced many famous artists and leaders who

have attained distinction in their professions. Seminole journalist and tribal leader Betty Mae Tiger Jumper, born in 1927, became the first woman elected to lead the tribal council for the Seminole Nation of Florida in 1967. In 1949, she had been the first Florida Seminole to graduate from

Buffalo Tiger, a former chief of the Miccosukee Seminoles in Florida, operates a gift shop and an air boat tour service in the Everglades.

high school. She founded a newspaper for the tribe in 1963 and became its editor. In 1997, the Native American Journalists Association honored her with its Lifetime Achievement Award.

Donald Fixico, born in 1951, is a Seminole who has achieved distinction as a professor of history, teaching at universities throughout the United States, and as director of the Indigenous Studies Program at the University of Kansas. He has published many books.

Jerome Tiger (1941–67), a Muskogee-Seminole raised in Oklahoma, is among the most famous Indian artists. His paintings portray events ranging from the Green Corn Ceremony, to the Trail of Tears, to contemporary Indian life. Seminoles have produced many other leaders, including sculptor Kelly Haney. He has been a leader of the Oklahoma State Senate for many years.

## The Seminoles' Future

In years to come, the Seminoles will continue making important contributions to the professions and the arts, and they will continue producing leaders to guide their people through the twenty-first century and beyond. As the Seminoles look to the future, they now have the advantage of being allowed to govern themselves. They now have a voice in their own destiny, and that is a big change from the recent past.

## ∿∿∿ The Oklahoma Capitol Dome ∿∿∿

Oklahoma recently placed a dome on top the state capitol building in Oklahoma City. The state commissioned Seminole sculptor Kelly Haney to create a large sculpture of an American Indian to put on top of the dome. Haney's sculpture is a Plains Indian warrior, ready for battle. The warrior's foot is tied to the ground, signifying that the warrior will not retreat. The statue was placed on top of the dome in the summer of 2002.

# Time Line

**about 1300**  High point of the mound-building civilizations of the Mississippi River Valley.

**1540s**  Spanish expedition of Hernando de Soto through Southeast.

**early 1700s**  European diseases and armies wipe out Florida Indians.

**1700s**  Muskogees (Creeks) who will become Seminoles move south into northern Florida; they are joined by runaway slaves; Seminole tribe formed.

**early 1800s**  Georgia slave owners invade northern Florida trying to recapture their runaway slaves.

**1815**  Many Muskogees who had been defeated by the U.S. in the War of 1812 flee to the Florida Seminoles; General Andrew Jackson attacks the Seminoles in Florida.

**1821**  American settlers begin pouring into Florida, driving the Seminoles to the south.

**1830**  Congress passes Indian Removal Act, allowing U.S. government to move Indians from their lands in the east to the west.

**1832**  Seminole removal treaty; many Seminoles are removed to Indian Territory (now Oklahoma).

**1835-42**  Seminole war in Florida.

**1855-58**  Last Seminole war in Florida; U.S gives up trying to remove all Seminoles, leaving two or three hundred in Florida.

**1861-65**  U.S. Civil War devastates Seminoles in Indian Territory.

**1880-90s**  Seminoles in Indian Territory forced to accept individual farms; most of their land is thrown open to white settlement.

**1907**  Seminole Nation is dissolved when Oklahoma becomes a state.

**early 1900s**  Seminoles do not benefit from oil boom in their homeland.

**1957**  Seminole Nation of Florida is formed, gains federal recognition.

**1962**  Miccosukee Indian Tribe of Florida gains federal recognition.

**1970s**  Seminoles in Oklahoma found new Seminole Nation.

**1980-90s**  Tribal businesses help provide tribal revenue and programs.

# Glossary

**ambush:** to capture or kill by trapping or lying in wait.

**Civil War:** the war between northern and southern U.S. states that lasted from 1861 to 1865.

**Confederate:** usually Southerners, the side that fought the federal government during the Civil war and tried to split the United States into two separate nations.

**clan:** a group of related families.

**constitution:** the basic laws and principles of a nation that outline the powers of the government and the rights of the people.

**custody:** the care and keeping of a person or thing.

**endurance:** the ability to do something for a long time.

**Everglades:** area of marshland or swamp, often under water and covered with tall grasses.

**fraud:** an act of tricking or cheating.

**medicine men:** religious leaders and healers.

**mound builders:** Indians in North America who built large earthen mounds for ceremonies, burials, and temples; ancestors of the Seminoles.

**nation:** people who have their own customs, laws, and land separate from other nations or peoples.

**negotiation:** talking to try to come to an agreement about differences.

**removal:** to move people from their homelands.

**stickball:** a ball game played with a stick and a ball about the size of a tennis ball.

**truce:** a short stop in fighting to allow both sides to try to come to a peaceful agreement.

**Union:** usually Northerners, the side that stayed loyal to the federal government during the Civil War.

# More Resources

## Web Sites:

**http://www.cowboy.net/native/seminole** Is the official web site of the Seminole Nation of Oklahoma.

**http://www.cviog.uga.edu/Projects/gainfo/seminole.htm** Will lead you to a number of sites on Seminoles.

**http://www.floridamemory.com/PhotographicCollection** Type the words *Seminole Indian* into this site's search engine and find hundreds of photos on Seminole life in Florida.

## Videos:

*America's Great Indian Nations.* Questar, 2002.

*Black Indians: An American Story.* Tapeworm, 2000.

*Black Warriors of the Seminole.* Ivy Classics, Inc., [No date].

*Seminole.* Schlessinger Media, 1993.

## Books:

Bial, Raymond. *The Seminole.* Marshall Cavendish, 2000.

Brooks, Barbara. *The Seminole* (Indian Tribes of America). Rourke Publications, 1990.

Jumper, Moses, and Ben Sonder. *Osceola: Patriot and Warrior.* Raintree Steck-Vaughn, 1992.

Kavasch, E. Barrie, Herman J. Viola, and Felix C. Lowe. *Seminoles* (Indian Nations Series). Raintree Steck-Vaughn, 2000.

Kidlinski, Kathleen V. *Night Bird: A Story of the Seminole Indians* (Once Upon America). Penguin Putnam Books for Young Readers, 1995.

Marvis, B. and Philip J. Koslow. *The Seminole Indians.* Chelsea House, 1994.

# Things to Think About and Do

## Different Kinds of Homes

Can you draw pictures of a log cabin and a Seminole chickee to show the differences in the two kinds of houses?

## A New Life

Imagine being moved from the swampland of Florida to the thickly wooded hills of Indian Territory. How would life be different? How would you adjust to the new surroundings? What new skills would you need to learn? Write an essay on what you imagine life would be like.

## The Few against the Many

Can you think of some reasons why a small group of Indians in the swamps could hold out against a large army that was trying to capture them? Explain your thinking in a few paragraphs.

# Index

African-Americans, 6, 7, 11
alligator wrestling, 23
American Civil War, 12
archery, 19

baskets, 24
Battle of Negro Fort, 7
beliefs, 19-21
Big Cypress Reservation, 18, 22
boat building, 16
businesses, 23, 25

chickee, 17
clothing, 4, 15, 24

Everglades, 8, 12, 16, 17

family life, 14-15
farming, 16
fishing, 16
Fixico, Donald, 27
Florida Annual Indian Arts
  Festival, 22

grave houses, 21
Green Corn Ceremony, 21, 23,
  27

Haney, Kelly, 27

Indian Removal Act, 8
Indian Territory, 8, 10, 12, 13

language, 5

medicine men, 20, 21, 25
Miccosukee Reservation, 22, 23,
  26
mounds, 5

oil, 25
origin story, 4
Osceola, 8, 9

reservations, 4, 12, 18, 20, 22, 23,
  24

Seminole Nation, 4, 13, 24-26
Seminole Nation Museum, 24
Seminole Negro Scouts, 11
Seminole Wars, 7, 8-9, 10-11
slaves, 6, 11
sports and games, 18-19
stickball (lacrosse), 18, 19
Stomp Dance, 25

Tiger, Jerome, 27
Tiger Jumper, Betty Mae, 26-27
Trail of Tears, 10, 27
Treaty of Paynes Landing, 8
tribal councils, 23, 25

Wildcat, 8, 13